Museum Kittens

Also Available:

The Midnight Visitor

Museum Kittens

The Mummy's Curse

by *Holly Webb*

Illustrated by *Sarah Lodge*

tiger tales

For my readers in St. Petersburg—H.W.

For Alby and Neri—S.L.

tiger tales

5 River Road, Suite 128, Wilton, CT 06897
Published in the United States 2021
Originally published in Great Britain 2020
by the Little Tiger Group
Text copyright © 2020 Holly Webb
Illustrations copyright © 2020 Sarah Lodge
Author photograph © Charlotte Knee Photography
ISBN-13: 978-1-68010-486-8
ISBN-10: 1-68010-486-1
Printed in the USA
STP/4800/0423/0821
All rights reserved
10 9 8 7 6 5 4 3 2 1

www.tigertalesbooks.com

Contents

Museum

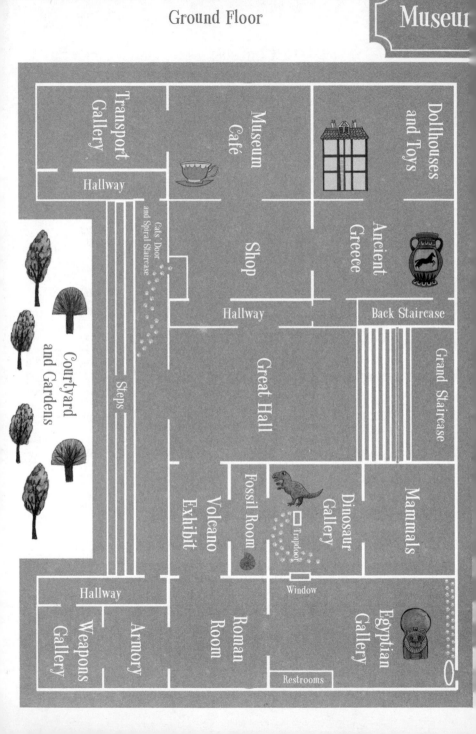

Transport Gallery

Hallway

Museum Café

Dollhouses and Toys

Ancient Greece

Shop

Cats' Door and Spiral Staircase

Hallway

Back Staircase

Courtyard and Gardens

Steps

Great Hall

Grand Staircase

Fossil Room

Dinosaur Gallery

Trapdoor

Mammals

Volcano Exhibit

Window

Hallway

Armory

Roman Room

Egyptian Gallery

Weapons Gallery

Restrooms

Russian Room

Hallway

Polynesian Gallery

China and Glass Room

Jewel Room

Japanese Gallery

Balcony

Hallway

Back Staircase

History of Cookery

Maritime Gallery

Temporary Exhibit

Costume Gallery

Regency Room

Window

Musical Instruments

Hallway

Ear Trumpet Collection*

Manuscript Room

Medieval Gallery

🐾 Chapter One 🐾

A Curious Delivery

"What are they all so excited about?" Boris whispered to Peter and his sisters. He was peering around the huge painted mummy case that hid the tunnel down to the basement, where the museum cats lived.

The Egyptian Gallery was full of museum staff talking in whispers as they opened up a large wooden crate and started to unwrap something that had been inside. The elderly professor who ran the Egyptology department was actually squeaking with delight.

"Is it jewels?" Bianca asked hopefully, pushing the large orange kitten out of the way so she could see.

"It could be one of those golden masks that the pharaohs had in their tombs," the small tabby Tasha suggested, slinking farther around the mummy case to look. "It must be something very special."

"Gold…," Bianca purred. "Diamonds, too? Maybe pearls?"

"I don't think so," said Tasha. "The masks are mostly gold and lapis lazuli— that beautiful blue stone. The ancient Egyptians used it a lot."

"Hmph! Blue stone." Bianca looked disappointed, and her white tail drooped. "Not as nice as diamonds. But I do like gold."

"*That* doesn't look like a jeweled golden *anything*," Peter pointed out. The black kitten had given up trying to see around Boris and crawled underneath him instead. "It's just … a piece of paper."

"Huh? That's not a treasure!" Bianca said, annoyed.

"What are you looking at?"

All four kittens skittered sideways in surprise as Grandpa Ivan appeared behind them. He was the oldest of the cats, white and long-haired with a great drooping mustache of whiskers. His ears looked chewed, and he only had one eye. But he knew everything that was going on in the museum, and he was very good at sneaking up on the kittens. "Ah, it's here!"

"Do you know what it is?" Boris asked. "It doesn't look very exciting, but the museum people are making a big deal about it. They're putting it in an enormous glass case. Look!"

"It's a temporary loan from a museum on the other side of the country," Grandpa

Ivan explained. "They're rebuilding their Egyptian Galleries, so they're lending out their precious exhibits. It's part of the *Book of the Dead*."

"The what?" Tasha squeaked.

"The *Book of the Dead*." Grandpa Ivan chuckled. "It's a set of ancient magic spells for how to safely get to the afterlife, written out on long strips of papyrus. That's paper made of reeds."

Tasha nodded intelligently, and the other kittens tried to look as though they knew what he meant, too. All four of them were gazing at the strange piece of paper in fascination. Ancient magic spells!

"The Egyptians used to put copies of it into people's tombs so the spirits would know what to do. The scrolls were expensive, though, so they were mostly made for royalty and important officials. This one came from the tomb of a pharaoh, Thutmose I, so it's very grand, with beautiful pictures. This isn't the whole thing, of course. Only a little bit of the scroll is left. All of the tombs were raided by thieves many times— and you can imagine that a long roll of papyrus is quite delicate."

"Hang on…. This is a list of instructions for *ghosts*?" Boris looked shocked.

"Mmm, not quite. I think they'd only be ghosts if they got it wrong," Grandpa Ivan said thoughtfully. "Although no one is quite sure where Thutmose I's body ended up…. He had at least three different coffins. But what's really special about this piece of papyrus is that no one knows what it means. Most of the *Book of the Dead* has been translated—it's all written in hieroglyphics. Picture writing. But this part of the book is tricky to read, apparently, and this is the only copy that's ever been found! I heard the staff talking about it in the café. They're pretty sure it's a spell that has something to do with a magical amulet—or it could be a curse on anyone who steals it…."

"I don't like the sound of that," Peter muttered, his whiskers shivering. "What if it's bad luck for it to be here in the museum?"

"There's no such thing as bad luck!" Tasha gave him a grown-up kind of look. No one was exactly sure how old Peter was. He had been left at the museum as an orphan, so the other kittens liked to think he was the youngest. "Spells and curses are all nonsense. And even if they weren't, this one is thousands of years old! Its power must have run out by now."

"Or it has spent years and years getting worse and worse," Boris growled, and Peter nodded at him, wide-eyed.

Tasha sighed. Really, the other kittens were all so superstitious. She knew there was absolutely nothing to be worried about.

On the other side of the gallery, someone else was eyeing the new exhibit, too. Four rats were peeking out of a hole in the skirting board. It was a very small hole, and they had to keep elbowing each other out of the way.

"What do you think it is?"

"Dunno, but it's got to be something good. Look at that case! Look how thick the glass is!"

"Definitely special. See all the fuss they're making? And did you see those horrible cats over there? Behind the mummy? They have their eyes on it, too."

"Hey, let me take a look! Do you think it's something especially *delicious*?"

"Has to be. And look, you can see it's all nibbled around the edges. Someone's already had a taste."

The rat leader nodded. "Well, there we are," he said, looking at them all. "We can't let those mangy cats have it then, can we? We'd better start coming up with a plan…."

News of the special new exhibit in the Egyptian Gallery began to spread around the museum. And so did rumors about the curse.

The truck that had brought the old artifacts to the museum had gotten two flat tires and experienced mysterious engine failure on the way, the café staff muttered.

Then the day after the papyrus arrived, one of the guards slipped in the gallery and banged his head on the display case. He said he didn't know how he'd done it—he was fine one minute and on the floor the next. All the water pipes started to make strange whistling noises, and there were eerie shrieking sounds whenever anyone flushed the toilet in the bathrooms by the Egyptian Gallery.

The day after that, children on a field trip came to visit, and one of the children threw up all over the floor. The cleaners said there was *definitely* a curse.

"I told you," Peter whispered to Tasha as they sat watching the others practice hunting one evening after the museum had closed. "That papyrus is bad news. The pharaoh doesn't like it being here!

Grandpa Ivan said no one knows where Thutmose I's mummy ended up, and I bet his ghost is furious! Something really awful is going to happen to the museum!"

"No, it isn't," Tasha said, rolling her eyes. "Is it my turn yet?" she added, twitching her tail. But Boris was already creeping forward in a hunting crouch.

"Very good," Grandpa Ivan growled. "And wait … wait and watch…. Don't spring…. I said *don't* spring!"

Boris tumbled head over heels and landed with a meaty thump. Then he glared at the others. Bianca was smirking, and he could tell Tasha and Peter were trying not to laugh. Peter's black muzzle was all wrinkled up with the strain of holding the laughter in.

"Are you all right, dear?" their mother, Smokey, asked, nudging him gently.

"Yes," Boris muttered as he stood up. Why did being the biggest and strongest of the kittens always mean that he was the clumsiest, too? They were all supposed to be practicing their hunting skills so that they could grow up to be museum guard cats, like their mother and their grandfather and all their aunts and uncles. Boris knew that one of these days, he was going to be a mighty hunter. He just needed to grow into his paws first.

"Take a rest, Boris," Smokey said. "Tasha, you try. Imagine a huge gray rat, sneaking along the edge of the wall. You see him…."

Tasha tensed up, her ears pricking and her tail beginning to swish from side to side. Boris watched her slinking toward the imaginary rat and sighed. She looked so … *professional*. At the moment, it seemed like the only way *he'd* ever catch a rat would be if he fell on top of it.

Maybe it was because he'd eaten so much dinner, Boris thought sadly. He *was* very full—maybe that's why he was so clumsy. He wished they didn't have to have lessons in the evenings, but Ma and Grandpa Ivan wanted them to practice hunting in the galleries, where they would be real guard cats one day. So that meant they had to wait until the visitors had left.

Tasha prowled across the room, trying to imagine a rat, all sharp teeth and beady black eyes. Hunting imaginary rats was one thing, but the thought of facing off against a fully grown rat was terrifying. Boris said he'd seen rats that were twice her size.

"Keep low!"
her mother called,
and Tasha crouched down even
farther, paws trembling with the effort.

"Nicely done, nicely done," Grandpa
Ivan purred. "Very good form there,
small gray striped one."

"She's Tasha." Smokey let out a sigh.

"I know perfectly well who she is. Now,
back, back, as fast as you can!"

Tasha whirled around and shot across
the gallery, claws scratching on the
slippery floor. She just managed to skid
to a stop before she crashed into the
other kittens.

"Hmm. Yes. Good job." Grandpa
nodded regally, and Tasha glowed.
She wasn't used to being told she was

good at things—she usually got scolded for daydreaming during their hunting lessons. It was hard not to daydream when they were surrounded by so many beautiful things.

Peter prowled across the gallery to take his turn, and Tasha sat down and started to lick her paws and swipe them across her ears. Then she looked sideways at the tall plinth towering over them all.

The bronze statue of Bastet, the cat goddess, was one of her favorite museum treasures. It was more than two thousand years old, but the cat goddess looked just like so many cats that Tasha knew. On her best, cleanest days, Tasha hoped that she looked a little like the statue, too.

She had read the sign on the plinth, and she knew that Bastet was the Egyptian goddess of many things— secrets and songs and protection and happiness. But mostly cats.

"Thank you," Tasha whispered to the statue. "Did you help? I'm not usually very good at lessons."

The bronze cat stared silently ahead, and her gold earrings glittered in the dim light. Tasha wished that she wasn't in a glass case. The cat was old and precious and delicate, Tasha knew that, but it would be so wonderful to nuzzle up against her, just once. Tasha couldn't help feeling that Bastet's hard bronze skin would melt to soft tabby-brown fur, and she'd nudge back.

"You see, Boris," Tasha heard Grandpa Ivan say sternly. "Perfect hunting from little-black-kitten-I-can-never-remember-the-name-of. Practice! Practice, that's all it takes! Learn to control your paws!"

"Yes, Grandpa," Boris muttered, and Tasha gently brushed whiskers with him.

She didn't think Boris had been that bad.

"I'm always falling over my paws," she whispered to him.

"I've never been so hopeless before." Boris heaved a sigh. "I think it's that horrible piece of paper." He glared at the papyrus in its glass case. "It's cursed, all right."

"No, it isn't!" Tasha hissed, but then her whiskers twitched worriedly.

Something was wrong; she could feel it. Peter was marching proudly toward them across the gallery—but then his ears began to flatten back, and the fur stiffened up all along his spine.

There was a strange creaking noise, and somehow Peter's shining black fur seemed to turn gray all at once. Tasha looked up slowly toward the ceiling and saw a large, dark crack spread across the white plaster, branching out like the rivers on the maps she'd studied in the Map Room. Dust shimmered down like a waterfall.

"Run!" Boris yowled, and Peter scrambled out of the way just as the middle of the ceiling collapsed. Huge chunks of plaster crashed to the floor, right where he'd been standing.

"Peter!" Tasha meowed, nuzzling anxiously at him. And then she looked back at the gallery and whispered, "The treasures! Bastet's statue! The mummy cases! The papyrus!"

"All of you, out of here," Smokey hissed, herding the kittens to the safety of the doorway. They scurried along in front of her, glancing back at the scene of devastation, but it was hard to see anything through the haze of dust.

"Are you all right?" Boris asked Peter worriedly as Bianca tried to groom the dust out of his black fur. He was a small, skinny gray kitten instead of a small, skinny black kitten now.

"There's no point licking him," Grandpa Ivan told her. "What he needs is a bath."

Peter stared at Grandpa in alarm, but the old white cat was already thinking about more important things. "Where's that caretaker when we need him?" he muttered. "He should have come running…. Ah…."

Grandpa Ivan's whiskers bristled, and the kittens looked around to see the Night Guard hurrying through the Roman Room. He was carrying a radio, talking into it as he ran. He stopped in the doorway, staring at the pile of plaster with eyes as round as marbles.

"About time," Smokey muttered. "On your way, kittens. We don't want the Night Guard thinking we had anything to do with this."

"He already does," Peter whispered back.

"Look. He's glaring at us."

The three other kittens peered around and saw that Peter was right. The elderly caretaker was eyeing the cats suspiciously.

"How can he think we broke the ceiling?" Boris asked indignantly. Then he scowled at Tasha and the others, who were looking at each other meaningfully. "That's not fair! I've *never* broken a ceiling. It was only a small dinosaur. And we put it all back together before anyone noticed!"

🐾 Chapter Two 🐾

Watching

The Night Guard seemed to stare suspiciously at the kittens every time he saw them after that. And Boris was absolutely sure that they weren't given as much food as usual, either.

"There was hardly any breakfast!" he complained to Peter as they sneaked upstairs the next morning to spy on all the interesting goings-on in the Egyptian

Gallery. Tasha and Bianca had already hurried off to see what was happening. "No nice meaty pieces. Just that horrible brown kibble. He's paying us back because he thinks we did something to the ceiling. I told Tasha that papyrus was cursed! We have to do something now that it's spoiling our breakfast—the most important meal of the day! Things are getting really serious."

"It tasted all right to me," Peter said.

Boris shook his head sadly. Peter had arrived at the museum in the middle of a rainstorm a few weeks before. Until then, the black kitten had been living on the streets, and he'd always been hungry. Boris couldn't imagine what that would be like. But really, even a street cat should be able to tell the difference between lousy cat food and a tasty piece of fish.

Last night, whoever the Night Guard had been talking to on his radio had shown up in a hurry and brought a bunch of nervous people with clipboards. Grandpa Ivan had come back down to the basement looking worried.

"They're going to close the Egyptian Gallery and the Roman Room until the ceiling has been fixed," he'd explained to the other cats. The four kittens had curled up in their nest of old tapestries, pretending to be asleep but listening with all their ears.

There had been an anxious chorus of meows—the Egyptian Gallery was very popular with visitors. Shutting it down was going to make a lot of people really upset.

Now Boris and Peter crept under the portable screens that the museum staff had put up at the door between the Roman Room and the rest of the museum. There were all kinds of strange noises coming from the Egyptian Gallery—bangs and screeches and occasional shouting. It didn't sound like their museum at all. Usually an unruly school group was the noisiest it got.

"Ooooh, out of the way," Peter squeaked as the screen was pulled back, and two burly men staggered by. The two kittens squished themselves against the wall to avoid the men's stomping boots. The museum staff couldn't see above the huge box they were carrying.

"Where are they going with that?" Boris wondered.

"I guess they want to get the precious things out of the way," Peter said, peering thoughtfully across the Roman Room. "Do you think they're moving everything? Some of those mummy cases are huge. And what about that stone sarcophagus? They'd need a crane!"

"A crane...," Boris purred excitedly. "Do you think so? I've never seen a crane." Then he nudged Peter. "If they brought builders in to fix the ceiling, there could be all kinds of things! Drills! Cement mixers! Maybe an angle grinder!"

Peter stared at him. "I don't even know what that is."

Boris lowered his head. "It's for cutting things…. I like machines," he admitted.

"Mmm." Peter eyed the bustling scene in the Egyptian Gallery. "We'd better be careful. I don't think they're going to want us in there. And your mother did tell us to stay out of their way. She said everyone would be busy and we shouldn't bother them."

"I don't see why we can't be here," Boris said, but he didn't meet Peter's eyes. "We're only making sure no rats get in, aren't we? I wouldn't put anything past those nasty creatures. They're probably planning an attack on the mummies right this minute!"

He marched forward, tail high, and Peter sighed and scurried after him.

The Egyptian Gallery was full of people. The elderly professor was standing in the middle, directing her staff members who were frantically packing huge crates or putting wooden frames around the exhibits that were too big to move easily. They seemed to be clearing out the middle of the gallery under the fallen part of the ceiling. The kittens had seen most of the people from the museum before, from a distance, but there were strangers here, too. A big platform built of metal bars had appeared in the middle of the gallery and there were three builders in hard hats standing on it, staring at the ceiling.

"Scaffolding!" Boris gave a little purr

of bliss. "I've always wanted to go up scaffolding."

"How do you *know* all this stuff?" Peter asked.

Boris shrugged. "Well…. I like things that move and make noises and go fast…. Big things…." He looked longingly at the scaffolding again. "Do you think they'd let us go up there?"

"No." Peter shook his whiskers firmly.

"I guess you're right." Boris sighed. "Oh, well." Then his ears twitched, and he started forward. "Hey, look! It's Bianca. She's up there already!"

Peter's ears flickered worriedly. The white kitten was up on top of the scaffolding, winding herself around the ankles of a tall man

in a suit who was pointing out the big
hole in the ceiling to the builders. He
seemed to be telling them just how
serious the damage was, and they were
nodding and frowning. Eventually,
the tall man noticed Bianca. He stared
down at her as though he'd never seen
such a creature before.

It was very unusual. Bianca was very good at making people love her. The Night Guard *always* tickled her under the chin. Even though it was his job to take care of the museum cats, he could be very grumpy, and sometimes the cats thought he didn't like them very much. But Bianca always made him smile when she purred—which he certainly never did for any of the others.

"Who's that?" Peter whispered to Boris.

"The museum director. He's very serious. And very important."

The museum director glared at Bianca and sniffed. Then he sneezed, loudly. Another cloud of dust shimmered down from the ceiling, and the people on top of the scaffolding gave the hole worried looks.

The director muttered something and then picked Bianca up at arms' length—as though she smelled badly! He marched over to the ladder and handed her down to one of the museum staff members.

"They're throwing her out!" Boris whispered to Peter, laying his ears flat and edging back under a drop cloth.

Peter squished in next to him. "I don't believe it…."

Bianca didn't believe it, either. The museum worker hurried out with her and dumped her in the middle of the Roman Room. The white kitten stood there for a moment, her tail fluffed up like a brush. No one treated her like that! Not ever!

"She's furious," Peter breathed. He could see Tasha watching from behind a huge granite lion. She looked just as shocked as they were.

"We'd better not let her know we saw," Boris muttered. "She'd never forgive us."

They squished back against the wall and watched as Bianca stalked proudly out of the room, the fury crackling off her fur.

"Now that really is bad luck!" Boris said, shuddering. "We'd better find someone to tell her how beautiful she is. And fast."

"That's interesting," hissed a watching rat, his whiskers peeking around the side of a display case. "Very interesting indeed. That tall one is important. And he doesn't like those little cats. Not at all. And if there are no cats in the gallery…."

"Out we come!" squeaked the smaller rat from the other side of the case.

🐾 Chapter Three 🐾

Getting in the Way

Even after the builders had gotten
rid of Bianca, the other kittens kept
sneaking back to check up on the work
in the Egyptian Gallery that day. It was
fascinating—even more fascinating
because they weren't really supposed to
be there.

They had to stay out of the way of
all the staff and especially the museum

director, who was marching around and shouting at people. They kept on having to dodge Smokey and Grandpa Ivan and the other cats, too—no one seemed to want a bunch of kittens getting in the way. But Boris kept finding new power tools to drool over, and Tasha and Peter wanted to keep an eye on all the treasures up there with the dust and dirt and piles of plaster.

And to keep an eye on the rats.

Boris had been telling the others for a long time about the huge rats he'd seen in the tunnels and behind statues, and how he'd almost caught them. But now that the ceiling was down and the walls were full of cracks, there seemed to be scuttling noises and ratty whispers *everywhere.* The kittens were on edge all day. Peter felt as if he had to keep looking over his shoulder—and he was never quite sure if he was expecting a huge rat or an angry ancient Egyptian….

"You know, I don't think the builders actually like working in the museum," Tasha told the others at breakfast the next morning. Once again, they had only been given dry cat food, and Boris was eating it with a pained look.

"What do you mean?" Peter asked indignantly. Even though he was still new to being a museum cat, he felt very protective of his home.

"I heard one of them say that the Egyptian Gallery was spooky!" Tasha shook her head sadly.

The other three kittens stared at her.

"There's a haunted papyrus in there, Tasha!" Boris pointed out, licking crumbs off his whiskers. "Of course it's spooky! Look at everything that's gone wrong since it showed up. Plus, the gallery is full of enormous stone coffins!"

"That papyrus is not haunted!" Tasha adored living in the museum and finding out about all the exhibits—but even she was starting to feel doubtful about the

Book of the Dead. She shuffled her paws. "And the coffins and mummies are so beautiful…," she added, looking at them all. "You really think they're spooky? I mean, I guess the cat mummies are…."

"Ughhhh…," Bianca shuddered. "Don't talk about them. They make my whiskers twitch."

"And those jars!" Boris looked gloomily around the basement. The museum's collection of ancient canopic jars was lined up along one wall now. "It's making me not want to eat my breakfast, knowing that all those brains are over there."

"Not brains, Boris!" Tasha said, sounding shocked. "Only the stomachs, livers, lungs, and intestines went in the jars. The ancient Egyptians drained the brains out of people's noses and threw them away."

"You're not helping!" Boris stopped eating and sat back, gazing at his bowl sadly.

Tasha licked her nose and then stepped away from her bowl, too. "Yes. I'm not very hungry now, either. But we shouldn't be scared of them, you know. The bodies and—um—parts—they're all thousands of years old."

"Really old, powerful spooks, then!" Bianca shivered. "I'm not surprised the builders don't like being here. What if it's not just the curse on that papyrus? I bet the mummies are really annoyed with being disturbed, too. I bet they're furious!"

All four kittens looked sideways at the canopic jars and the painted mummy case that was now standing in the corner of the basement. Without realizing what they were doing, they edged a little closer so that they could feel the warmth of each other's fur.

"The ancient Egyptians really liked cats!" Tasha said firmly, but she was still pressed close against Peter. "They worshipped them! We're being silly."

Peter nodded. "Even if ghosts did start popping out of all those mummy cases, they'd *love* us."

"I think it's our duty to go and keep an eye on the builders," Boris said firmly. He glanced quickly at the jars again. "And I'd rather be up there than down here...."

The builders were hot and grumpy and annoyed. The hole in the ceiling had something to do with leaking water pipes, which made the plaster soggy. Every single one of the pipes had to be carefully checked to make sure they weren't rusting, and it looked like a long, tedious job. Plus, every time the builders turned around, there was someone from the museum panicking about them damaging the priceless treasures.

"This job is getting on my nerves," one of them muttered as they perched on the edge of a wooden crate to drink a bottle of water.

"Mr. Museum Director made very sure to tell us that there absolutely, definitely wasn't anything weird going on, didn't he?" his friend replied, glancing over his shoulder at the heavy glass case with the papyrus inside. It was just too solid to move out of the gallery. "The sooner we get out of here, the better."

"Let's stay out of their way," Tasha said as the four kittens peered out from under one of the drop cloths.

"Hmph." Bianca stuck her nose out and glared. "Horrible people!" She was still upset about being thrown out of the gallery the day before, but she'd finally come upstairs with the others because she hadn't wanted to be left alone in the basement. The carved faces on top of the canopic jars seemed to keep looking at her. All of the cats down there were asleep after their night shift guarding against the rats, and their basement home felt strangely quiet and empty.

One of the builders shuddered and nudged the other. "You see that? Those drop cloths are moving. I don't like this place. Gives me the heebie-jeebies."

"You're not the only one," his friend agreed. "Let's get on with those pipes."

"Gosh…." Boris edged out past Bianca. "Look at that. He has a blowtorch!"

"Boris, come back!" the others whispered.

But the orange kitten was entranced. The builders had gone back to cutting out the broken pieces of pipe now, and the blue flame of the blowtorch hissed and roared in the most exciting way. He padded over to look, darting from one shrouded plinth to another. But as he got closer to the builders and their tools, he was too interested to be careful.

"Boris! We're supposed to stay out of their way!" Tasha meowed worriedly.

"Look at him! He's right in the middle

of the gallery!" Peter squeaked. "They'll see him any minute!"

It would have been better if the builder with the blowtorch *had* seen Boris. As it was, when he switched off the blowtorch and stepped back to check how the pipe was looking, he fell right over the kitten instead.

Boris shot out of the gallery with a squeal, and the builder landed flat on his back in the middle of the floor. "What was that?" he yelled.

The other men were laughing too hard to answer him, but eventually one of them managed to explain that it was a cat.

The builder went on shouting about it for quite a while.

"I told you they were horrible," Bianca said smugly as the four kittens gathered in the Roman Room, listening to the stomping and yelling from inside the Egyptian Gallery.

"He sat on me! I was almost squashed flat!" Boris held up one shaking paw and then the other, gazing at them as if he thought they might fall off. "I mean, I know I'm accident-prone, but that man had a blowtorch! He could've set the whole museum on fire."

"He turned it off before he fell over you." Bianca rolled her eyes. "And actually, it was your fault."

"Was not!"

The white kitten shrugged, and Boris glanced at the others.

"It wasn't!" Boris insisted.

Tasha wrinkled her nose. "You did creep up behind him," she told her brother gently. "I don't see how he was supposed to know that you were there."

"*What* is going on here?" Grandpa Ivan stalked into the Roman Room with his fur all on end. It looked as though he'd been woken up from a nap. "I could hear the shouting three rooms away. Oh, it's *you* again…," he said, glaring at Boris. "What did you do this time?"

"I was only looking at the blowtorch," Boris said in a small voice.

"The *what*?" The fur lifted along Grandpa Ivan's spine, and he whipped around to stare at the Egyptian Gallery in alarm, obviously expecting flames to billow out any moment.

"It's all right. It was off when the man fell over Boris," Tasha explained helpfully.

"Oh my goodness," Grandpa Ivan growled. "Enough. I don't want to hear any more! You're confined to the basement, all of you! Downstairs, now, on the double!"

❧ Chapter Four ❧

A Rat!

The kittens spent the rest of the day holed
up in the basement, trying not to imagine
that the canopic jars were watching them.
Boris sat curled in a ball with his tail
over his ears, while Tasha and Peter were
trying their best to make him feel better.
Even Bianca was nicer to him than she
usually was. He looked so miserable.

Boris hardly even touched his dinner.

Afterward, Grandpa Ivan and Smokey sat the kittens down in one of the few clear spaces left in the basement. The museum cats who weren't on watch were gathered around them in a circle.

"Are we being banished from the museum?" Peter squeaked to Tasha.

"No! At least … I don't think so," she whispered back, but her ears were flattened down. How much trouble were they really in?

"You four…," Grandpa Ivan began, glaring at them.

Boris jumped up. "I'm sorry! It was all my fault!" he rambled. "Please don't be angry with Tasha and Bianca and Peter. I only wanted to see how a blowtorch worked."

Smokey sighed, and Grandpa Ivan said, "Hmph!" All of the cats sitting around them seemed to shift and stretch. Suddenly, the underground room felt warmer.

"You are an absolute nuisance," Smokey told her biggest kitten, but then she licked his ears so it didn't seem as though she were really that upset.

"Those kittens need something to do," one of the other cats suggested. He was a long-legged tabby with thickly marked dark stripes over a brownish coat and bright yellow eyes. "They're getting older. They should be too busy to fool around, tripping up builders."

"We don't fool around," Tasha said to Peter under her breath.

"Can we guard the Egyptian Gallery? Please?" Boris begged. "The rats have it staked out. We keep hearing them! I'm sure they're after that papyrus, or maybe the builders' lunches…."

The other three kittens nodded eagerly.

The dark-striped tabby cat looked thoughtful. "I have noticed quite a few rats close to the Egyptian Gallery when

I've been on my shift."

The other museum cats began to mumble.

"Mm-hmm."

"We could use some extra lookouts…."

"Those rats are getting too comfortable."

"And the kittens *have* been improving their hunting skills," Smokey put in.

Grandpa Ivan looked grim. "Very well then. Tonight, you can have your first shift as museum cats." He eyed the four of them fiercely. "You'd better not let me down!"

Tasha was keeping watch from a wooden crate next to the statue of Bastet. She was sitting tall, her head held high like the cat goddess. She knew she was only a scruffy tabby kitten, and not an Egyptian goddess—but tonight, she was guarding the gallery!

The kittens were under strict orders to watch for rats creeping in through any of the huge holes that the builders had made in the walls, the floor, the ceiling…. But so far, no one had seen anything.

The goddess statue seemed to be staring at the glass case with the papyrus, and Tasha

55

stared at it, too. The drop cloth covering the case had slipped a little, and she could see the picture writing—strange little squiggles and figures. Except … she could make out some of the pictures. If she squinted sideways, wasn't that faded scribble there a cat? There was definitely a cat in the little painting in the corner, too. She needed to take a good look later. Maybe if there was a curse, they could find out how to get rid of it….

Tasha leaned out around the plinth to catch Boris's eye. "Anything?" she mouthed.

Boris shook his head. He was just as
proud of their new job as Tasha was,
but he'd been hoping for a little more
excitement. He huffed out a sigh and
fixed his eyes back on the hole in the wall
he was supposed to be guarding.

It was a very boring hole.

So boring that he kept imagining little
ratty whiskers poking through it. There
they were again. Every time he looked
closer, they turned out to be dust or a
trick of the light. Boris narrowed his eyes
and glared at the whiskers.

This time, they didn't disappear. In fact,
they came a little closer, and behind them
was a pinkish ratty nose.

"There's a … there's a—" Boris let out
a stifled meow. Now that the big moment

had finally arrived, he was just too shocked to say anything. "Rat … rat!" Boris whispered. "There's a rat! Oh, my!"

The rat smirked at him. No, it full-on *grinned*. Obviously, it could see that Boris didn't know what to do.

"Hello, small cat…," it hissed.

"I am *not* small!" Boris hissed back. He was a lot bigger than the rat, for starters. Furious, he charged head-on at the hole, and the surprised rat shot back inside the wall again as Boris thumped into him.

"Boris! Boris!" The other kittens hurried over.

"Are you all right?" Peter asked worriedly. "You hit the wall!"

"There … was … a … rat!" Boris mumbled. His head was spinning a little, but he blinked hard and peered back at the others. "I chased away a rat. I really did. It had whiskers…."

"A real one?" Tasha gasped. They had been told about rats so often, but this was the first time any of them had actually chased one.

"We should tell Ma!" Bianca cried. "I'll
go!" She darted away, a little white shape
shooting through the drop cloths.

Boris attempted to focus—there
seemed to be too many kittens in front of
him. Tasha and Peter leaned against him,
lovingly propping him up.

"A real rat…," he muttered.

Inside a battered old piece of guttering
on the outside wall of the museum, the
rat that Boris had chased sat nursing his
whiskers. "They're everywhere," he hissed
to the rest of his group. "Little, furry,
striped cats. Little nuisances. I thought
that tall man had gotten rid of them at

last, but they're still all over the place and growing bigger every day!" He twitched his whiskers and groaned. "My nose will never be the same again. It could be broken!"

"Stop whining, Luther," another rat muttered. "So we can't get back in through that hole now. We should have made an all-out assault last night, like I told you! But you insisted on having a celebration cheese sandwich party behind the café garbage cans instead. What about going through the wall on the other side?"

"They have those small cats watching

everywhere now, Morris, I tell you! Ow, my nose!"

"They really don't want us getting our paws on that wonderful piece of paper," Morris said resentfully.

"What about the pipes?" suggested a small brown rat, and the others turned to stare at her.

"What *about* the pipes, Dusty?"

"Well, that's why there are holes in the walls. Those builders have found cracks in the pipes, and that's what made the ceiling fall down. They turned off all the water now, right?"

"What does that have to do with anything?" Luther growled. His sore nose was making him very bad-tempered. Plus, he was still embarrassed about being chased off by a kitten.

"If the pipes are so old and rusty and thin that they need builders to fix them, why shouldn't *we* scramble along inside the pipe and nibble through?" the little brown rat suggested, her eyes bright with excitement. "It wouldn't be hard. Not if we all took turns. And if we nibbled a hole in exactly the right place, we could come out of the pipe next to the glass case with that special delicious-looking paper."

"Hmmm." The other rats looked thoughtful.

"We'd have to make sure we were in the right pipe," Dusty added. "We can't get turned around and end up in the wrong one, or we'll get soaked."

"Yes, of course." Luther sat up and sniffed, and then clapped a paw to his nose. "Easy. Oh, it's almost in our claws, my dears. The dinner to end all dinners!"

🐾 Chapter Five 🐾

A Strange Dream

"Those little cats are still there!" Luther muttered as the group of rats peered through their nibbled hole later that night. They had managed to chew through the pipe and then the drywall in just the right place, and Dusty was looking very pleased with herself. "All over the gallery. Look, there's the white one, curled up in the drop cloths on top of that wooden crate. The little cats are usually tucked in bed in the basement by now."

"That paper must be really special if they're leaving cats here to guard it overnight," Dusty said, leaning out of the rusty pipe.

"How are we going to get to it?" Morris asked, eyeing the chunky glass case below.

Dusty turned back, looking worried. "Hmm…. You're right. It is a little—um—solid, isn't it?"

"Exactly," said Morris, looking smug. He didn't like it when Dusty was more clever than he was.

"What's so special about that piece of paper?" asked Pip, the youngest rat, who wasn't usually brave enough to say anything.

The other rats looked at him witheringly.

"It's very old," said Morris.

"And—um—special…," said Dusty.

Luther heaved a huge sigh. "Are you telling me that we can't get in that case, and even if we could, it's just a piece of old paper?"

"Um. Maybe?" Morris shifted his paws nervously, hoping Luther wasn't going to have one of his tantrums. "I don't know why the cats are making such a big deal about it, to be honest."

"They do like old things…." Dusty sighed. "The whole building is full of old stuff. I don't understand cats, I really don't."

"Or people." All the rats shook their heads sadly. Then Dusty twitched her whiskers.

"There's a noise...."

"Little cats snoring?" Luther smirked. "Some guards they are. That white one is definitely asleep."

"No.... A kind of ... *wet* noise."

"Wet? Like ... watery?" The rats looked around worriedly. They had been very careful. They had come out in just the right spot. The water had definitely been turned off.

Hadn't it?

"Yes!" squealed Dusty as the watery noises grew louder. "Run!"

As the night wore on, the kittens were taking turns keeping watch so that the others could take a catnap. Tasha stretched out her paws, snuggled deeper into her nest of drop cloths, and dreamed….

She was walking down a dry and dusty path. It was so hot! The sun blazed down on her tabby fur, and the grasses by the side of the path buzzed with sleepy insects.

On the other side of the path the river ran, greenish-brown and sleepy, too—it was hardly moving. Out in the middle of the water, there was a boat with a square yellowish sail and men heaving at the oars.

In that strange way of dreams, Tasha
knew that she was far from home, but it
seemed like she was in the right place.
Somehow, it was important that she was
here....

A small girl in a long white dress
came walking along the path in the other
direction and stopped to pet her. She
crouched down and made a fuss of Tasha,
rubbing her ears and tickling her under
her chin. It was just the kind of treatment
that Bianca usually got, and when the little
girl went on her way at last, Tasha purred
softly to herself. This was a good place.

As Tasha walked on, she realized that
the river was now higher up the bank than
it had been before the little girl stopped. It
wasn't far from her paws. She looked back

and saw that the child was running now, chasing after her mother, who was calling out to her anxiously.

Tasha eyed the water uncertainly. Was it supposed to do that? It seemed to be rising very fast. Maybe she should get off the path. But the land all around seemed to be so flat. If the river was flooding, it would spread all across those fields of wheat. Tasha felt her tail fluff out. She scurried along the path, faster and faster, but it only seemed to be stretching out in front of her.

There was another cat with her now, running, too. At first, Tasha thought that it was Ma, as the cat was bigger than she was and dark-furred. But then she saw that the stranger's fur was a true midnight-black, darker even than Peter's black coat. Her eyes were a clear bright gold, and she wore a golden collar.

A strangely familiar collar.

"Wake up, little one," someone whispered on a purr, and Tasha blinked.

It had been a dream! Only a dream! Her heart was thudding so hard, it almost hurt. She felt as though she really had been running along that dusty path. Tasha gasped in a deep breath and tried to shake the threads of sleep away. It was dark in the gallery now, and she couldn't see any of the others. They must be hidden among the drop cloths somewhere. Bianca was supposed to be awake, since she was on first watch. After an hour, she was supposed to wake Boris.

Tasha nodded to herself. She would go and talk to Bianca about her odd dream. Probably Bianca would tell her how silly she was being, and for once, Tasha wouldn't mind her sister being rude.

She stretched, ready to get up, and realized that her tail was damp. *The river*, she thought sleepily. *I must have trailed it in the river.* She shivered, still half caught in her dream.

There was no river. She was in the gallery.

But her tail was definitely wet.

Tasha sat up slowly and peered around, trying to focus in the green emergency lighting. The floor of the gallery was moving. Rippling, almost. And it seemed to be a lot closer to her than it had been when she went to sleep.

55

Tasha felt the fur stand up all along her spine. The floor of the gallery was covered in deep, dark water!

Chapter Six

Sound the Alarm!

"Wake up, all of you!" Tasha meowed. "Wake up! The gallery is flooded! There's water everywhere!" Now that she was fully awake, she could hear the water gushing from a broken pipe. It sounded as though it was flowing very fast.

"What?" A dark head popped up in the shadows, and Tasha saw the light flash in Peter's green eyes. He was curled up on top of one of the display cabinets, and Tasha watched him lean over and stare down at the water slopping around the floor.

"It's still pouring in," Tasha called. "I can see it now. It's coming out of that pipe just behind the papyrus case. It's getting higher!"

"It can't be." Bianca stood up, yawning and shaking her head. "That's ridiculous. The water was turned off because of the construction. It's absolutely impossible for the gallery to be flooded."

"You jump in it, then!" Tasha hissed furiously. "Go on. If there's no water there, why don't you just jump down?" She glared at her sister.

Bianca eyed the water and took a step back. "Well. Maybe there is *some* water down there," she admitted. "I guess the builders must have finished working on the pipes and turned it back on."

"The floodwater is halfway up the cabinets," Tasha growled. "It will be over our heads soon!" Then she let out a little meow of alarm. "The treasures! The ancient Egyptian treasures—they can't get wet. The papyrus! It's priceless—it's the only copy!" She shuddered, looking around at the dark water. "The pharaoh *must* have put a curse on it. I believe it now...."

"Typical," Bianca muttered. "Just like you to be more worried about the museum stuff than you are about us!"

"We're museum cats, Bianca!" Tasha gave her a shocked look. "We're supposed to be guarding the gallery. And now it's flooded, *on our watch*." She didn't add, *And you were supposed to have stayed awake.* It would be mean.

"Where's Boris?" Bianca said quickly. Clearly she was trying to change the subject, but she was right to be worried.

"Boris! Where are you?" Tasha said.

No answer.

"Boris? Are you all right?" Peter called anxiously.

"He's probably still asleep." Bianca sniffed. "BORIS!"

The three kittens heard a muffled groan and then a faint rustling, as if Boris were waking up and stretching. "Shh, Bianca, I'm sleeping. It's the middle of the night! What are you waking me up for?"

"Because there's a flood!" Bianca yowled.

"Where is he? Can't he see all the water?" Peter gazed around the gallery, trying to pinpoint Boris from his voice. "Oh, there he is! He's on the end of the same cabinet as me…. Boris, no!"

"Stay still!" Tasha yelped. "Don't do that!"

But it was too late. Boris was stretching and yawning and rolling right off the side of the display case.

"Help!" he yowled frantically, flailing his paws and twisting himself away from the water.

Peter dashed across the display case to grab him. He caught Boris by the scruff of his neck, but the orange kitten was so much bigger than Peter, and the glass display case was so slippery….

"I'm falling!" Peter hissed desperately.

Luckily, Tasha and Bianca had already leaped across from the wooden crate to help. Together, the three of them dragged Boris back onto the top of the display cabinet.

All four kittens sat there shivering and panting and staring at the water.

"Thanks…." Boris coughed. "Thanks, everyone. Why is it always me?"

No one said anything. It always was….

"Let's get out of here," Bianca said, her tail swishing back and forth. "I can feel my fur frizzing in the dampness."

"I don't know how we can get out," Peter said. "The builders shut the doors to the Roman Gallery when they left, and the tunnel down to the basement must be underwater by now."

"Do you think the basement is flooding, too?" Tasha asked, her ears flattening. All those cats, fast asleep…. Ma was down there, and Grandpa Ivan! "We need to sound the alarm," she meowed.

"But how? Who's going to hear us from up here?" Bianca huddled closer. She looked terrified, as though she were beginning to realize how much danger they were in.

"We could put a message

in a bottle and float it on the water," Tasha said, peering down at the water sloshing against the display case. It was still rising— just like in her dream.

"Except we don't have a bottle. Or any paper. Or anything to write with!" Bianca snapped.

"I'm sorry…. It's what they do in adventure stories." Tasha swallowed hard. She'd always wanted to have an adventure, but she'd thought it would be more fun. And not as wet.

"The guard cats on their rounds might hear us if we meow very loudly," Peter suggested. "Or maybe the Night Guard. Except … I wish those doors weren't closed. They're very solid."

Boris looked around. "There *is* a

window up there. Not a big one—just the long gap that lets in the light from the Dinosaur Gallery. Someone might hear us through that." He nuzzled Tasha's ears and whispered, "I thought the bottle was a good idea." Then he sat up straighter, turning to the others. "So let's try. Ready?"

All four kittens raised their heads and meowed, wailing an alarm call across the dark water and hoping that there was someone out there to hear.

Chapter Seven

Water Everywhere

Boris waited for the echoes of their frightened meowing to die away. "Can you hear anything?"

The kittens sat, their ears pricked. But except for the steady sound of pouring water, the museum was silent all around them.

"Let's call again…," said Boris. He was trying to sound calm and confident, but they could all see that the water was gradually rising up the side of the cabinet. What would they do when it reached the top? "Ready?"

They yowled as loudly as they could, but there was still no answer.

"This is no good!" Bianca said, stomping up and down the glass-topped case. "No one's coming, and the water is getting higher and higher! We'll have to swim for it, and I don't think I can swim!"

"Me, neither," Tasha said in a tiny meow.

"Don't panic," Boris said. But he couldn't think of a good reason why they shouldn't. "We have to keep on calling. We can't just … stop."

"What are you little ones doing down there?" came a disapproving voice, and the kittens whirled around.

Behind them, high up in the wall, was a small metal grille, which was the cover to a ventilation shaft. The museum was full of odd tunnels and tubes, which the cats—and the rats—used as pathways. A white paw unhooked the grille, and Grandpa Ivan peered down at the kittens. "What exactly is going on?"

"There's a flood, Grandpa!" Tasha called. "I was dreaming about the Nile River. And then I woke up, and my tail was soaked!"

"The pipes are leaking again," Boris put in. "It wasn't us, though! At least, I'm pretty sure it wasn't," he added. "I think I'd know if I'd flooded the whole gallery...."

"Probably that group of damp and panicked-looking rats that shot past me a couple of hours ago." Grandpa Ivan sighed. "I knew I should have chased after them and found out what they'd been up to. But the old legs weren't quite up to it."

"Rats! Of course!" Tasha cried and glanced at the others. "I told you there wasn't a curse!"

"It doesn't matter about the rats, Grandpa. You have to come and rescue us!" wailed Bianca. "There's so much water! I don't like it!"

"Yes, yes, okay," Grandpa Ivan muttered. "Don't get your whiskers in a knot. I'm coming. Just a minute.

Now...." He edged a little farther out of the ventilation shaft, pressing his front paws against the wall. "Hmm. If I'm careful, I can...." He leaped down onto the nearest wooden crate. "Oooof. Old paws...."

"Grandpa!" the kittens squeaked and meowed, padding their paws lovingly up and down on the glass case. "You did it!"

"Mmm...." Grandpa Ivan sighed as he eyed the dark water uncomfortably. "I did, didn't I.... But was that the right thing to do? There's the question."

"What do you mean?" Tasha asked.

"You're still over *there,* and I'm still over *here,* small tabby one." Grandpa Ivan came slowly to the edge of the wooden crate. "I'm not sure I can get to you. And you certainly can't jump far enough to get to me."

His voice sounded faint and shaky, and Tasha suddenly remembered that Grandpa Ivan had come to the museum as a kitten after he'd been rescued from the river. A little girl had found the half-drowned white kitten tied up in a sack. His owners hadn't wanted him, and they'd thrown him in the water. It was only luck that had let him wash up on the riverbank.

"Grandpa, don't lean out so far!" she called across the gallery. "Don't look at the water like that. Please don't!"

"What is it?" Boris muttered. "What's wrong with him?"

"Remember the story he told us?"

Tasha whispered. "About the farm and the people thinking he was no use because a lot of white cats are deaf? They threw him in the river! I don't think he likes water—look at him. It's making him all … strange…. Grandpa Ivan, step back!" she meowed.

But the old white cat seemed to be mesmerized by the slowly shifting water. He was leaning out farther and farther.

"He's going to fall in!" Peter gasped.

"We can't let him." Boris marched to the other side of the glass case and padded his paws against the smooth surface. There wasn't much grip, but he'd have to do the best he could.

"What are you doing?" Bianca shrieked. "You can't jump that far!"

"Someone has to," Boris said grimly. "And my legs are the longest. We can't leave him there—he's going to topple in any minute! Get back. Stay out of my way. I need to get a running start."

The other three kittens watched wide-eyed as Boris raced across the cabinet and launched himself out across the water.

"Please make it, please make it, please make it," Tasha mumbled.

With a scratch and a thump, Boris

landed solidly next to Grandpa Ivan, who stepped back on top of the case, shaking his white head.

"What was I doing?" he muttered. "Very odd...."

"It was the water, Grandpa," Boris explained. "I think you were remembering...." He trailed off, not knowing quite what to say.

"Yes. Yes, I think you're right." Grandpa Ivan shivered and then straightened himself, glaring across the water at Peter, Tasha, and Bianca. "Okay. We'd better get back over there."

"Do you think you can?" Tasha called anxiously. "It's a long way."

"Nonsense!" Grandpa Ivan's whiskers bristled. "Perfectly capable. Life in the old cat yet. Leave us room to land, everyone. Come along, young one. Together. On three?"

Boris nodded, and the white cat and the orange kitten stood next to each other. "One, two, three…."

They ran and leaped, paws outstretched, sailing over the gap.

"There!" Grandpa Ivan gasped. "There,

you see? Good work, young one. Very good work." He licked the top of Boris's head, and Boris sat down beside him, proudly tall.

"Now what are we going to do?" Bianca demanded, looking up at Grandpa Ivan. "We're still here, and so is all that water."

"Yes, yes, indeed it is," Grandpa Ivan said thoughtfully. "So. No obvious way out. The doors through to the Roman Room are shut, which is a good thing I guess, since they're nice and solid. They're probably keeping most of the water trapped in here."

"But what if it's pouring down into the basement?" Tasha said worriedly. "The tunnel behind the mummy case will be completely underwater."

"Hmm. Maybe some water will have gotten through," Grandpa Ivan agreed. "But that tunnel doesn't go straight down, does it? It dips in the middle and goes back up around another set of pipes. Whole place is riddled with old pipes, which is what caused the problem in the first place. Most likely a lot of the water is caught in that dip and hasn't reached the basement yet." He sighed. "And that's a shame, in a way. If the other cats knew there was a flood, they'd be right up here to see what was going on."

"So no one is coming to rescue us?" Bianca asked shakily.

Grandpa Ivan sniffed. "Museum cats are perfectly capable of rescuing themselves!"

🐾 Chapter Eight 🐾

A Great Idea

"There is that funny long window." Boris walked to the edge of the display cabinet and nodded at the gap that opened into the Dinosaur Gallery. "If only we could get to it...."

"Could we jump across?" Tasha suggested, eyeing the various cabinets and boxes scattered around the edges of the gallery. "Like stepping stones."

Boris peered thoughtfully at the water. "I don't think so. There's a big space in the middle where they cleared everything out because of the collapsed ceiling. I wish they hadn't taken the scaffolding away."

"I'm not swimming," Bianca said. "I can't jump into that water. I'll sink!" Then she looked ashamed of herself and added, "I'm sorry, Grandpa. I shouldn't have said that. It'll be all right...." But she didn't sound very sure.

Grandpa Ivan nudged her gently. "I'm not liking the idea of jumping in, either. There must be some other way."

Tasha frowned, looking around at the flooded gallery. The water sloshing against the side of their cabinet made her think of her dream, the river suddenly rising and washing away the path. The dream had started so nicely, with the boat sailing by and the little girl making such a fuss of her.

"A boat!" she squeaked. "We need a boat!"

Boris looked at her helplessly. "There's a clay one in the cabinet underneath us," he admitted. "But I don't see how we can get it out. And it's not big enough for all of us."

"I'm not convinced it's going to float, either," Peter said, peering down between his paws. "I don't think it's meant for actual boating."

"I didn't mean that one!" Tasha sighed. "Isn't there anything we can make a boat out of? Or a raft? What about the pieces of wood from all these wooden crates?"

The cats gazed at the sturdy, solid boxes and wrinkled their noses doubtfully. It didn't look like it was going to be easy to pull off any pieces.

"This is where it would be really useful for me to know more about power tools," Boris said to Grandpa Ivan.

The old white cat turned around and glared at him with his one eye.

"Well, maybe not," Boris said hastily. "So, any other ideas?"

Tasha stiffened, and her ears pricked forward with excitement. "Yes," she breathed. "Look! That!"

Grandpa Ivan and the three other kittens gazed out across the water in the direction she was looking.

"What is it?" Boris asked, puzzled. "I can't see anything."

"That's because you can't see it against the dark water," Tasha said excitedly. "Look, right there! And it's floating toward us! That sign! Can you see it?"

She was right. A flat black board was floating lazily across the gallery, sloshing and slipping in the water.

"No food or drink in the gallery," Boris spelled out slowly, and then he gave a little snort of laughter. "A little late now."

"You want us to get on *that*?" Bianca asked, horrified.

"There isn't anything else," Tasha told her gently. "The water is rising. If we all get on, we can paddle it across to the gap in the wall and jump through."

"Paddle," Bianca said faintly. "Oh, my whiskers!"

"We have to!" Tasha said. "If the water rises much farther, the treasures in the cases are going to be damaged. We have to protect them—it's what we *do*."

"Small tabby one is right," Grandpa Ivan muttered. "Think of those painted wooden mummy cases. The pharaoh's papyrus! And the sarcophagi! And the mummies themselves! Thousands of years old! They're not going to be waterlogged on my watch."

He crouched down, ready to reach out and snag the sign with one long paw. "Don't look at me like that," he muttered to the kittens. "I can feel you staring. Perfectly all right. Lot of nonsense, being scared of water. There we go, you see?" he said triumphantly, hauling the board in against their glass case. "Got it!"

"You should get on first, Grandpa," Boris said. "You're the heaviest. You sit in the middle, and we'll spread out around the edges to balance it out."

Grandpa Ivan wriggled forward and put his other front paw down onto the sign. It rocked wildly, and water sloshed over the top. Bianca gave a little meow of fright.

"You're going to have to get wet, Bianca," Tasha said, losing her patience. "You either climb on the raft and get a little wet, or you stay here and get *very* wet."

Bianca stared at her sister, her mouth open. Tasha didn't often argue, but now her green eyes were emerald-glittery, and her whiskers were bristling. The white kitten nodded meekly and stepped to the edge of the cabinet, leaning down to look at the makeshift raft. She flinched a little as Grandpa Ivan settled in the middle of the board and more water came over the edge, but she didn't say anything.

"One at a time," Grandpa Ivan said. "Slowly, slowly. Peter, come on."

The black kitten closed his eyes for a second and then hopped onto the board, pressing up against Grandpa Ivan. "It's all right," he told the others breathlessly. "Just a little wobbly."

"Now you, Bianca." Boris and Tasha nodded to each other. They wanted her on the raft before she got all panicky again.

But Bianca had clearly decided to be brave. She jumped down before she had to be pushed and stalked around to the other side of the board to balance Peter out. There she sat, looking queenly.

Tasha shivered. Since Bianca hadn't made a fuss, she couldn't, either. She really didn't like the way the board kept shifting and the water rippled across it. But this had all been her idea. Quickly, before she could think about it too much, she hopped down onto the raft. It shook underneath her, and she spread out her paws for balance.

"Boris!" Grandpa Ivan commanded. "Jump on. Let's get out of here."

Boris sprang onto the board, and it dipped down for a moment before righting itself again. "Oops, I'm sorry," Boris muttered. "Okay! We're all here!"

Grandpa Ivan leaned forward, his ears flattened and purposeful. "Paddle!" he roared.

It was harder than it sounded.

"You're going in circles!" Bianca complained. "Ooooh, don't *splash* me!"

"We're not doing it on purpose," Tasha growled back. "It's difficult! You paddle, too, and don't just sit there. And we're not going in circles. I'm sure we're closer to that window than we were before."

"A little," Boris agreed. "Hang on. I have an idea." He crept to the back of the raft and wriggled down flat, letting his tail trail into the water. "Ugghhh, it's cold," he muttered. "All right. Let's see if this works." And he began to swish his tail back and forth like a long, orange paddle.

"We're moving, we're moving!" Tasha
squeaked. "Keep going, Boris!"

"A little cat engine," Grandpa Ivan
chuckled to himself. "Good work, orange
one. We're getting there."

With the other three kittens paddling at
the sides, and Grandpa Ivan paddling with
both front paws over the front, soon the
sign was bumping up against the gap in
the wall.

"One at a time, one at a time!" Grandpa
Ivan called. "Be careful—don't let it
wobble. Oooof, I'm stiff. Pull me up,
kittens!"

And then there they all were, sitting
in a line on the edge of the gap and
looking down at the delightfully
dry Dinosaur Gallery.

❧ Chapter Nine ❧

The Night Guard

Luckily, there was a solid fiberglass model of a *Stegosaurus* close to the opening that the cats could clamber down. Boris wasn't sure he could face another encounter with a dinosaur skeleton. There were just too many little pieces to put back afterward.

"Now what do we do?" Tasha said after they'd finished nudging and nuzzling at each other. Bianca was sitting underneath the *Stegosaurus*, trying to lick her fur back into shape, and Peter was shaking his ears, which still felt full of water.

"We must wake the cat guard!" Grandpa Ivan said, stamping one paw.

"Well, yes. But shouldn't we try to find the Night Guard, too?" Tasha pointed out. "We need him to turn off the water."

"Yes," muttered Grandpa Ivan. "The dampness is getting to me. Yes, at once!"

"Where is he usually now?" Boris wondered.

Grandpa Ivan's muzzle wrinkled as he thought. "He does his rounds, and then he takes a nap on the seat of one of the carriages in the Transport Gallery. Then

he comes here, to the dinosaurs,
to eat his sandwiches. Then another
nap on the couch in the Regency
Room."

"He should be there then, right?" Peter
said. "It feels late enough. Up to the first
floor, everyone!"

The four kittens darted through the
Dinosaur Gallery and out past the
volcano exhibit to the Great Hall and
the staircase. Grandpa Ivan lumbered
after them at the pace of an elderly cat
who had already been considerably more
adventurous in one night than he had
been in years.

"There he is!" Tasha hissed as
they skidded to a halt on the finely
woven carpet of the Regency Room.

It was set up to look as though several early nineteenth century ladies were having a tea party, although the tea was disappointingly fake—Boris had checked a long time ago. Three mannequins in long, embroidered dresses were posed as if they were chatting over the plaster cupcakes, but there was one elegant velvet couch that was usually empty.

Now, the Night Guard was stretched out on it, snoring gently.

"How do we wake him up?" Peter asked, looking up at the large man in dismay. "It was hard enough to wake up Boris. And even then, he almost fell in the water."

"Don't remind me," Boris muttered.

"I think Bianca should do it," Tasha said.

"The Night Guard likes her. If one of us wakes him up, he'll be grumpy."

The others muttered in agreement and stood back as Bianca stalked across the carpet toward the beautiful couch. She hesitated for a moment, and then jumped up onto the edge of the seat. She stretched out one delicate white paw and patted the Night Guard's face, just above his mustache.

Nothing happened, so Bianca tried again, patting a little harder.

This time, the Night Guard grunted and shifted on the couch, almost knocking Bianca off. She scrambled back up, squeaking angrily, and smacked his face hard with her paw.

"Watch it!" Boris muttered. "We want him in a good mood."

The Night Guard jumped up from the couch like an angry walrus, making snuffling, roaring sounds. He peered down at Grandpa Ivan and the kittens.

"Cats! Again! I might have known. Shoo! Go away!"

"I don't know why the museum gets him to take care of us when he doesn't even like cats," Tasha said, annoyed.

"Bianca! Be nice—do your thing!"

"I'm trying," Bianca hissed. She padded along the couch and jumped up onto its arm, ducking her head and purring and making little meowing noises.

"Yes, yes," the Night Guard muttered, petting her. "Yes, you're very pretty. Good kitten. Go away now. I need my sleep."

"Oh, honestly," Bianca said irritably. "Can't he see that it's important? Come on." She reached out, took the sleeve of the Night Guard's shirt in her teeth, and pulled.

He gave a start of surprise. "What is it? Are you hungry? It's a few hours until breakfast time, little one."

Bianca pulled at his shirt again and

then meowed frantically, running back and forth along the arm of the couch.

"That's it! He's listening," Grandpa Ivan called. "Keep going, Bianca! Jump down and see if you can get him to follow you."

Bianca sprang down onto the carpet and pulled at the Night Guard's pant leg. Then she darted away a few steps, gazing at him anxiously.

"What is the matter with you?" he mumbled, looking down at her in confusion. "Usually you just want me to pet you...."

Bianca dashed back and pulled at him again, and then she meowed at the others. "You do it, too! Pull him!"

Grandpa Ivan looked doubtful for a

moment, as if it was beneath his dignity to go pulling at a museum guard's pant leg. But then he sighed and came to join in.

The Night Guard looked down in amazement as four kittens and one elderly white cat took hold of his pant legs and tried to drag him toward the door. "All right, all right. I don't know what's going on here…. All right! I'm coming…."

Grandpa Ivan and the kittens got into position around him. Boris and Tasha dashed ahead, and Peter and Bianca walked beside each leg, ready to pull at his pants if he slowed down. Grandpa Ivan trotted behind, nudging the Night Guard in the back of the legs every so often to make him hurry up.

The Night Guard seemed bewildered by
the whole thing. Every time they passed a
door that led to another gallery, he seemed
to be considering making a run for it.

When they got to the top of the stairs,
he froze, grabbing the banister and shaking
his head. "No, no, no, no, no. NO! You'll
trip me up! I don't know what's going on
here. I really don't!"

The cats looked at each other helplessly.

"Could we push him down the stairs?" Boris suggested.

"Don't even think about it," snapped Grandpa Ivan. "Humans aren't like cats. They don't bounce, and they only have one life."

Bianca hissed with frustration. "I got wet! My fur is ruined! Ruined! I'm not doing all that for nothing." She sprang forward, catching her claws in the Night Guard's pant legs and climbing up to stand on his shoulder. There she nuzzled his cheek, purring and meowing, until the Night Guard reached up to pet her. He looked as if he didn't really want to, but he couldn't help himself.

"Walk down the stairs," Bianca meowed. "All of you! Walk down and keep looking back at him. Flutter your whiskers. *Try* to look sweet. Do the best you can, anyway."

"Sweet, is it?" Grandpa Ivan growled. "That young lady is much too full of herself, if you ask me. Come on, kittens." He began to stalk down the stairs, turning back every few steps to give the Night Guard a fearsome, full-teeth grin.

"Not like that…." Bianca heaved a sigh. But the Night Guard seemed to be so taken aback by Grandpa Ivan's one-eyed stare that he hurried down the stairs after him.

"Yes! Come on!" Peter, Boris, and Tasha raced down the marble staircase, leading the Night Guard past the volcano exhibit to the Dinosaur Gallery. There they leaped onto the *Stegosaurus* model again— ignoring the Night Guard's cry of alarm— and clambered up to the gap in the wall.

"Oh! The water has risen so much," Tasha gasped. "It'll be pouring through the doors into the Roman Room any minute."

"Can he see?" Boris looked back at the Night Guard. "Come here! Come and look!"

Grandpa Ivan headbutted the Night Guard in the back of the legs again, and the guard stumbled up onto the *Stegosaurus*'s plinth. The cats made a space for him to look through, and the Night Guard leaned forward to peer over the edge of the gap.

What he said next made Grandpa Ivan curl his whiskers and glare at the kittens. "It's lucky you that haven't been around people long enough to understand that." He bounded up to the ledge beside them and sighed. "But I think he's probably right."

The cats watched as the Night Guard stumbled away to turn off the water, muttering into his radio.

"Calling for back-up. Good, good," Grandpa Ivan said approvingly. "We'd better do the same. Emergency call to all the guard cats—we need to check the status of the basement. We might be flooded out any minute if the water has gotten through the tunnel. And who knows what the rats are doing. Fleeing a sinking ship, hopefully, but you never know."

"Sinking?" Tasha whispered, and the kittens stared at Grandpa Ivan worriedly. Did he think that the museum was doomed?

"No, no, I don't mean it like that. It's what rats do—they run. Whereas cats like us stay and help." Grandpa Ivan sighed. "Okay. Peter and Tasha—you run through the rest of the galleries. Tell the cats on watch what happened. Tell them to keep an eye out for any drips or splashes or strange noises in the walls. We don't know exactly what those rats did to the pipes. Boris and Bianca—come with me. We need to wake up everyone in the basement and warn them about the water. We may have to block up the tunnel until the gallery has been pumped out."

"Pumped out?" Boris asked hopefully. "With a pump? A really big one? Maybe even attached to a truck?"

"Just get down to the basement," Grandpa Ivan growled. "Sound the alarm!"

🐾 Chapter Ten 🐾

Saving the Treasures

Grandpa Ivan was right about the sloping part of the tunnel down to the basement—it had caught a lot of the water. In fact, the dip in the tunnel had turned into a kitten-sized swimming pool, but none of the kittens felt very much like trying it out.

When Boris and Bianca had raced into the basement and woken the other cats, they'd found that only a little water had overflowed and seeped down the rest of the hallway. Smokey had already organized the other cats into sopping it up with some old, moldy curtains that she had found in a box.

The precious Egyptian treasures in the basement had escaped any damage, but the gallery was ruined. Several members of the Egyptology department were in tears as they surveyed the damage early the next morning. The elderly professor had to sit down on the *Stegosaurus*'s plinth, with Grandpa Ivan in her lap. She had been at the museum for almost as long as he had, and she was very fond of him. Grandpa Ivan didn't usually sit on laps, but as he told the kittens afterward, sometimes it was necessary.

No one was going to be able to see exactly how bad the damage was until all the water had been pumped out and they could get inside. The kittens sat on a wall in the yard and watched as an enormous machine arrived. It was pulled by a tractor, which Boris thought was even better than a truck.

"Look at the size of those wheels," he said blissfully as it rolled around the side of the building in the dawn light. "They have to be almost as tall as the driver."

"Please don't go anywhere near it, Boris," Tasha pleaded. "Just remember that man with the blowtorch."

Boris's lip curled for a moment, but then he sat down and wrapped his tail tightly around his paws as if to stop himself from trotting over to the pump. He wasn't really sure what he could do to break an enormous tractor, but Tasha was right. He did seem to be a little unlucky around these things. It was very sad.

Still, right now, it was more important to make sure that the Egyptian treasures were rescued from the floodwater. He could investigate pumps later.

"Oh, it's working!" Tasha nudged him. "Look at the pipe!"

The water was pulsing along the rubber pipe that snaked out of the window and through the museum grounds, all the way to the river. The four kittens watched it hopefully. The water seemed to be moving along pretty well. Maybe the flood wasn't such a disaster after all.

The Night Guard was standing and watching the pipe, too, and for once, he didn't glare at the kittens when he saw them. He looked thoughtfully at them instead and clumsily patted Tasha on the head. "Good little cat," he muttered. "You all saved the day. Would you like some fish for breakfast?"

But when they sneaked in around
the elderly professor's ankles later that
day, even the kittens could tell that the
gallery was in awful shape. There were
brownish-yellow water stains around
all the white plinths, and the smell was
terrible.

"What about the treasures?" Tasha
asked worriedly, peering at the sodden
drop cloths around the display case
that held the pharaoh's papyrus. It was
just underneath the broken pipe. The
professor was pulling the sheet away, her
face pale with worry.

"Did the water get in?" Peter
demanded, stretching up to see. "Oh, it

couldn't have. She's smiling!"

"Such good luck!" Tasha breathed.
"I mean, obviously it would be better
if there hadn't been a flood at all. But I
guess at least this way, they'll check all
the pipes. None of the other galleries
will ever be damaged like this."

"Grandpa thinks it was the rats who broke the pipe, remember? He said he saw them running away looking guilty," Peter said. "It's a good thing that we're official museum guard cats now."

Tasha padded over to the tall plinth with the statue of Bastet and looked up at the bronze cat goddess with her golden collar.

"Were you watching over the gallery?" she whispered, trying to peer into the goddess's golden eyes. "Did you save all of the treasures? You wouldn't want all of your things to be ruined, would you?" She wrinkled her nose thoughtfully. "I'm sure I saw a painting of a cat on that papyrus. It's true, isn't it? There is no curse after all…."

Tasha was almost sure that she heard the very faintest purr, just for a moment. She wondered if it was Bianca, but the white kitten was over by the door, having her ears tickled by the professor. None of the other cats was anywhere near.

"Was that … you?" Tasha whispered hopefully to the statue. "You know, I don't think your paws were like that before," she added, swallowing hard. "They were farther apart. I'm sure of it. And your tail wasn't so tightly curled. I've looked at you a lot…."

The statue stayed still, gazing silently out across the damp gallery. But Tasha was sure her golden eyes glinted, and there was that faint breath of a purr again.

She *remembered* that purr.

Her dream! The black cat with the golden eyes had purred just like that when she told Tasha to wake up.

"And I woke up and woke the others, and we found the Night Guard," Tasha said slowly, figuring it all out in her head. "It wasn't just my wet tail that woke me—it was you! The black cat in

my dream had a golden collar on, just
like yours, and the most beautiful golden
eyes. You *were* watching over the gallery.
You sent us to help…. Us kittens." She
turned around, ready to race and tell the
others.

But then she stopped and looked back.
The statue was so still and so grand.
Would they believe her? Maybe they'd say
it was just a strange dream. She couldn't
bear it if they laughed….

"What are you thinking
about?"
Boris asked, casually
licking Tasha's ear,
when the others
came to find her a
few minutes later.

"Oh … just Egypt…," Tasha told him, with a secret little purr.

Boris nodded. "You know, it's very lucky that you woke up in time," he said.

Peter looked around at the water stains and the muddy, silted floor. "Yes, because the gallery could have been ruined."

"*We* might not have gotten out," Bianca added with a shudder.

"But we did. Someone made sure of that!" Tasha rubbed her chin lovingly against her sister's. And high above the four kittens, the cat goddess looked out over her gallery, her golden eyes shining.

Cats and Curses

The *Book of the Dead* does have cats in it! The sun god Ra could take the form of a cat named Mau (the sound that the ancient Egyptians thought cats made, like meow!). Mau fought with the monstrous snake god Apep, who represents evil. This story is in a part of the *Book of the Dead* that explains the different gods and goddesses. It was supposed to help the spirit of the dead person in case he or she met any gods on the journey through the Underworld.

There are many stories about curses on the tombs of the pharaohs, but as Tasha says, they're made up! Some Egyptian tombs did have curses written outside of them, but it wasn't very common. The most famous curse story is about the tomb of

Tutankhamen, one of the richest and most beautiful burial sites in Egypt, which was excavated by Howard Carter and his team in 1922.

Shortly after the tomb was opened, a messenger arrived at Carter's house and saw a cobra eating Carter's pet canary! Cobras were the symbol of the pharaohs, and the cobra symbol was often worn on royal crowns. The story of the poor canary was immediately written up in the newspapers, and many people believed that Tutankhamen had cursed Carter for opening up his tomb.

Several members of Carter's team did die over the next few years, but Carter himself died at age 64, 17 years later, and many of the people who were there when the tomb opened lived long lives.

Today, people can visit Tutankhamen's tomb
in the Valley of the Kings, near Luxor, which is
where Thutmose I's tomb can also be found.

Read the first book in the series!

The Midnight Visitor

HOLLY
WEBB

Holly Webb started out as a children's
book editor, and wrote her first series for
the publisher she worked for. She has been
writing ever since, with more than 100 books
to her name. Holly lives in England with her
husband, three children, and several cats who
are always nosing around when she is trying to
type on her laptop.

For more information
about Holly Webb visit:

www.holly-webb.com
www.tigertalesbooks.com